The Dog That Called the Pitch

Other books in this series:

MATT CHRISTOPHER

The Dog That Called the Pitch

Illustrated by Daniel Vasconcellos

Little, Brown and Company

Boston   New York   Toronto   London

Text copyright © 1998 by Matthew F. Christopher

Illustrations copyright © 1998 by Daniel Vasconcellos

First Edition

Library of Congress Cataloging-in-Publication Data

Christopher, Matt.
    The dog that called the pitch / Matt Christopher ; illustrated by Daniel Vasconcellos. —1st ed.
      p.   cm.
    Summary: Mike and his dog, Harry, the Airedale with ESP, are shocked to discover that the new umpire for Mike's baseball games can hear their mental conversations.
    ISBN 0-316-14207-7
    [1. Dogs—Fiction.   2. Extrasensory perception—Fiction.
3. Baseball—Fiction.]   I. Vasconcellos, Daniel, ill.   II. Title.
PZ7.C458Dm 1998
[Fic]—DC21   97-28224

10 9 8 7 6 5 4 3 2 1

WOR

Published simultaneously in Canada
by Little, Brown & Company (Canada) Limited

Printed in the United States of America

To Jackson Peters —M. C.

To my children, Nora and Davis —D. V.

"Please, Dad? Please?" Mike Barron stood in front of his father, holding a baseball and glove. "I haven't touched a baseball in a week!"

"Three days, liar," a voice rang out loud and clear in his head.

Mike's eyes shot across the lawn to his dog, Harry. Mike and Harry shared a special relationship. They could read each other's minds. Ever since Mike had brought Harry home from the pet shop, they had been best friends.

But sometimes Harry butted in when Mike didn't want him to. Like now!

"Keep out of this, nosy," Mike shot back. Harry chuckled.

Mr. Barron folded the newspaper he had

been reading and stretched. "Think you'll be pitching this week?" he asked.

"Omar is on vacation, so I guess I will be," Mike replied. Mike was a member of the Grand Avenue Giants baseball team. Usually he played second base. But sometimes Coach Wilson put him on the mound. "Could you catch for me for a while?"

"Tell him he needs the exercise," Harry suggested. "He ate the rest of the pie last night. He'll blow up like a balloon if he's not careful!"

Mike laughed. Mr. Barron was in great shape. Mike knew Harry was grumbling because he had hoped to get a piece of pie himself.

"What's the joke?" his father asked.

"Nothing," Mike said. "So, will you play catch with me?"

"If someone will fetch me my glove, sure."

Mike glanced at Harry. "Don't look at me," Harry said, turning up his nose. "I only fetch sticks and tennis balls."

Mike hurried to the garage, dug out his father's mitt, and returned to the front yard. Mr. Barron tugged on the glove and squatted down.

"Not too hard," Harry warned as Mike zipped in a fast one that cut sharply to the right. "Work on your control."

Mike threw in another. It was better than the

first pitch, but still a little off. So was the third throw.

"Ball, ball, ball," Harry said. "That's what I'd be calling them if I was the ump."

"Well, you're not, so pipe down!" Mike said out loud.

"What's that, son?" Mr. Barron asked.

"Uh, nothing," Mike said. "Just talking to myself."

"Heh-heh," came Harry's doggish chuckle.

"What's so funny?" a new voice boomed. Mr. Barron, Mike, and Harry all turned to see a man sitting behind the wheel of a red pickup truck. He wore glasses and had a huge handle-bar mustache.

"Well, if it isn't Charlie Grimley!" Mr. Barron cried. "What are you doing in town?"

6

Mr. Grimley hopped out of the truck and joined them on the lawn. "I'm the home plate umpire for the Grand Avenue Giants–Jaguar Stars baseball game today."

Harry chuckled. "Guess I won't be able to yell out, 'The ump needs glasses!' when you pitch today!" he joked to Mike. "He's already got 'em!"

Mr. Grimley glanced at Harry. "Never had any complaints about my calls," he said.

Harry gave a surprised woof. Mike's heart skipped a beat.

"Did Mr. Grimley hear you?" Mike wondered to Harry.

"Nothing wrong with my ears, either." Mr. Grimley's voice echoed in Mike's head. Harry's eyebrows shot up, so Mike knew he had heard it, too. Mr. Grimley could read their minds!

Mr. Grimley chuckled. Out loud, he said, "Well, I guess I'll see you all at the ballpark later on. I look forward to seeing you pitch, Mike." He climbed back into his truck and drove off.

"How did he know you were pitching, Mike?" Mr. Barron asked.

Mike gulped. "Uh, I dunno," he mumbled. Harry couldn't stop laughing.

"You squirt, Harry!" Mike scolded. "You want to get us in trouble?"

Harry looked up at Mike innocently. "Me? A troublemaker?" He chuckled again.

After thirty minutes of playing catch, Mr. Barron called it quits. Mike went inside to change for the game. He had mixed feelings about pitching today. He sort of wished that Coach Wilson would have Russ Crawford, also a righty, pitch. He wasn't sure he had the stuff to do well against the Jaguar Stars.

"Oh, you'll do fine," came Harry's reassuring

10

voice. "I'll be right there with you, don't forget."

"You better be," Mike answered.

Three o'clock came, and Mike rode to the game with his mother, father, and Harry. Not to have Harry with him would be like going outside in just his underwear.

Coach Wilson, wearing his usual baseball cap with the G on it and his Giants sweatshirt, gave his team a pep talk.

"I want you all to do your best today. Because who's going to win?"

"We are!" everyone in a Giants uniform, and one four-footed fan, yelled.

"Play ball!" came the call to start the game.

The Grand Avenue Giants had first bats. "C'mon, Frank! Blast it, pal!" yelled someone in the stands. The leadoff batter, Frank Tuttle, stepped to the plate. He took a mighty swing at Andy Hooten's first pitch but missed it by a mile. Luckily, he drilled the next pitch through short for a single.

Sam Button, batting second, grounded a single through the infield, advancing Frank to second.

"Score 'em, Jerry! Send it over the fence!" came cries from the fans.

Jerry Moon hit a grounder to second. Double play! Both Jerry and Sam were out. Frank held up at third base.

Moe Shinn got up. Andy Hooten got two

balls and two strikes on him, then struck him out.

"Way to go, Andy!" the Jaguar Stars dugout yelled.

The teams exchanged sides.

Mike pulled on his glove and headed toward the pitcher's mound. He was nervous.

"Keep cool," Harry told him. "You'll do okay."

Mike smiled. He stepped to the mound, tossed some warm-up pitches to Drew Ferris, then got ready for the Jaguar Stars' leadoff batter, Jody Sands. She looked too tiny to knock the ball out of the infield, let alone out of the park. But that was what she almost did as she swung at Mike's first pitch.

The ball sailed out to the right field fence,

where Bo Shinanski leaped
and caught it.
One out.

But Mike was nervous. He threw four balls and Wally Mills walked. Then Marsha Kerns got a double that sent Wally to third. Ray Feenie kept up the streak by driving a pitch over second. Wally scored, but Marsha was tagged out at third.

Tommy Aiken popped out on Mike's first pitch. The first inning was over.

Jaguar Stars 1, Grand Avenue Giants 0.

Catcher Drew Ferris got on base when shortstop Tommy Aiken made an error. But Mike popped out, and both Bo Shinanski and Travis Bass struck out.

The Stars picked up another run in the bottom of the second. In the top of the third, Russ Crawford, playing second base for the Giants, started off with a double to left center. The Grand Avenue Giants were on a roll!

Frank doubled, the next three batters walked, and Drew singled. Mike got up again and blasted a home run! The inning ended with the Giants having racked up seven runs.

But the Stars weren't about to quit. They picked up five runs in the next two innings. At the top of the sixth, the score read 7–7.

"Don't worry, Mike. You guys can take 'em. Grab a quick drink of water and get ready for your turn at bat," Harry said. Mike turned to give Harry the thumbs-up sign as he hurried out of the dugout toward the water cooler.

Too late, he heard Harry yell, "Watch out!"

Wham!

Mike collided with Mr. Grimley and—
crunch!—heard the sickening sound of glass
breaking beneath his feet.

Mike had stepped on Mr. Grimley's glasses
—and broken them!

"Oh, no!" Mike, Mr. Grimley, and Harry
moaned in unison.

"I—I don't know if I can
call the rest of the game
without my glasses!"
Mr. Grimley said as
he bent to pick up
the broken pieces.

"We'll have to call it quits until another day."

Mike groaned.

Harry cleared his throat. "I have an idea," he said. "Mike, did anyone else see what happened?"

"I don't think so."

"Mr. Grimley, do you want to continue with this game?"

Mr. Grimley nodded. "But how?"

"Mr. Grimley, get into position and keep your ears, er, your mind open."

Mike watched as his fuzzy Airedale crawled out from under the bench and disappeared behind the home plate backstop. Two seconds later, he saw a little black nose and two floppy ears peep through the fencing.

I wonder what he's got up his furry sleeve now? Mike thought.

A moment later he found out. Andy Hooten reared back and threw his first pitch to Bo Shinanski. It was headed for the middle of the plate but at the last second veered outside.

"Ball!" came Harry's voice loud and clear. And a split second later, Mr. Grimley's voice called out, "Ball!"

Harry was calling the pitches!

Bo got a single. As Travis prepared to bat, Mike had to say something to Harry.

"Just be sure to call them straight. No funny business to help out the Giants. We'll win it fair and square or not at all. Deal?"

"Deal," Harry replied.

Travis singled. With two men on, Russ Crawford poled a double, sending Bo home. The Giants were up by a run!

But that was all they could do that inning. Mike gathered his glove and headed toward the mound.

He sure felt strange, knowing that his dog was going to be calling the pitches!

He threw his first pitch. Jody swung hard but missed.

"Strike one!"

"Didn't need my help to make that call," said Harry with a chuckle.

Mike pitched again. This time Jody clipped the ball, but it rolled foul.

"Strike two!"

Jody missed the third pitch, too. One out. Two to go.

Wally Mills was up. He drilled a single over the shortstop's head. Marsha Kerns copied his move, sending Wally to second and landing on first herself. Two runners on, and only one out!

Then Ray Feenie hit a grounder right to Russ
Crawford at second base. Russ stepped on the
bag and got Marsha out, then threw to first for
the double play.

The throw was wild! Ray, one of the Stars' fastest runners, rounded first base and headed full steam ahead for second. Safe! Wally stayed at third.

Two players on, two outs.

C'mon, Mike said to himself. Just three strikes and the game's over!

But instead of three strikes, he heard Harry and Mr. Grimley call out three balls. It looked like Tommy Aiken was going to get a free ride to first.

Drew Ferris called time and trotted out to the mound. "We need a strike, Mike," he said. "A ball will load the bases. And look who's coming up."

Mike saw one of the Stars' best hitters, Mark Bradley, warming up in the on-deck circle. If Tommy got a walk, there was a good chance Mark would get a solid hit, maybe even a home run—and the Stars would take the game!

Mike took a deep breath and pitched. As he let the ball go, his heart fluttered. He couldn't tell if it was good or not. Tommy let it go by. Mike waited for the call.

"Strike!" said Harry and Mr. Grimley.

"Two more like that, Mike!" Harry added.

On the next pitch, Tommy pulled his bat back and swung as hard as he could.

He missed!

"Strike two!"

The Giants fans cheered loudly.

Mike got ready for his next pitch. He held the ball behind him, then started his windup. Legs and arms flying, he let it go!

His heart sank. He could see it was going to miss the plate by a mile.

But Tommy Aiken seemed determined to get on base by hitting, not by walking. He swung.

The bat clipped the ball and sent it in a high arc straight up into the air.

"I've got it!" Mike yelled. He rushed forward, his eyes never leaving the ball. Down it fell until—*plop!*—it landed smack in the palm of his glove.

"Out!" cried Harry and Mr. Grimley.

The Giants swarmed Mike. Harry rushed

out from behind the backstop and, with a
mighty leap, jumped into Mike's arms.

"You did it! Good game, buddy!"

"You too, fuzz-face!" Mike said happily.

Then he added, "Harry, if Tommy hadn't swung at that last pitch, would you have called it a ball or a strike? I mean, a strike would have won us the game, you know."

Harry's eyes twinkled. "When I saw where that ball was headed," he said with a devilish grin, "I decided to let Mr. Grimley call that one on his own! I mean, let's face it. Who'd believe a mutt like me could call the pitch?"